Cassie
Loves a Parade

I wish, I wish
With all *my* heart
To fly with dragons
In a land apart.

A Random House Pictureback® Shape Book
Adapted by Irene Trimble
Based on a story by Bob Carrau
Illustrated by Don Williams

CTW Books

Text and illustrations copyright © 2000 Children's Television Workshop (CTW). Dragon Tales logo and characters ™ & © 2000 Children's Television Workshop/Columbia TriStar Television Distribution. All rights reserved under International and Pan-American Copyright Conventions. Published in the United States by Random House, Inc., New York, and simultaneously in Canada by Random House of Canada Limited, Toronto, in conjunction with Children's Television Workshop. CTW Books is a trademark and service mark of Children's Television Workshop.

Library of Congress Catalog Card Number: 99-66226 ISBN: 0-375-80547-8
www.randomhouse.com/ctwbooks
Visit Dragon Land at www.ctw.org
Printed in the United States of America March 2000 10 9 8 7 6 5 4 3 2 1

One wonderful day, as Max was making make-believe milkshakes, his big sister Emmy spotted a shimmering glow in their playroom. "Look!" cried Emmy. "The dragons are calling!"

That glow was coming from Max and Emmy's most special treasure—an enchanted dragon scale they had found on the first day in their new home.

"Let's go, Max!" cried Emmy. And in a twirl and a swirl of sparkles, the magical scale spun them faster and faster, off to a magical place called...

Dragon Land!

"Wow!" Emmy beamed as she watched big and busy dragons hanging banners and decorating floats. Dragon Land was even more colorful than usual! "It looks like everybody is getting ready for a big parade!"

"That's right!" cried Ord, their big blue dragon friend. Ord gave Max and Emmy a huge, dragon-sized hug. "Today is the School in the Sky Parade, and Quetzal is just about to choose the names of the lucky dragons who get to ride on the floats!"

"I'm hoping Quetzal will pick me," added Cassie, the smallest and shyest of all the dragons.

Everyone eagerly gathered around Quetzal. They all crossed their fingers, toes, and claws for luck. Then the wise old dragon slowly began to pick the names of the winners out of his huge hat. Cassie closed her eyes, hoping with all her heart. She held her dragon breath as the names were read.

"The winners are…"

"Luna and Sparkle!"

"I didn't get picked," Cassie whispered as her heart fell. She just couldn't believe it. "I didn't get picked!"

"Uh-oh," said Ord. He knew that when Cassie was sad, she could shrink just as small as she felt. And sure enough, Cassie was soon the size of a dragonfly. She fluttered at the tip of Ord's nose for a moment, then flew off.

"Come back!" called Ord, but Cassie disappeared into a deep forest.

Cassie flew as fast as she could, big dragon tears filling her eyes. So it was no surprise when all of a sudden–*boing!*–she bounced off a spiderweb and landed, *plop,* on the ground!

"I hate today!" moaned the little dragon. "I wanted to be picked for the parade so-o-o much."

"Me, too," said a sad voice above her head.

Cassie looked up. The voice was coming from a drooping flower—a drooping dragon daisy, to be exact.

"My name is Cosmo," the flower snuffled sadly. "All my flower friends were picked to be in the parade. But nobody picked me."

Cassie hugged Cosmo. His tickly leaves squeezed her right back. "Thanks. I feel much better now," said Cassie. In a blink, she grew back to normal dragon size. "Sometimes I get little when I feel really bad about something," Cassie explained, wiping her eyes.

"I know just what you mean," Cosmo answered with a sigh.

Meanwhile, Emmy, Max, and Ord were soaring high above Dragon Land. They were desperately looking for Cassie. Zak and Wheezie, their two-headed dragon friend, had joined in the search, too.

"There she is!" Wheezie cried, spotting the pink dragon below. Emmy and Max held on tight as they all flew in for a landing.

"Why aren't you at the big parade?" Cassie asked with a little sniffle.
"Oh, it just wouldn't be any fun without you, Cassie," said Zak.

After Cassie told her friends Cosmo's sad story, Emmy came up with a shining idea. "Let's make a float and have our own parade! We could all be in it!"

"Sure!" Ord agreed. "I've got lots of things in my pouch to make a neat float!"

Soon everyone was very busy building a beautiful dragon float. Cassie worked hardest of all. When it was almost done, Ord reached deep into his pouch and pulled out a sparkly crown. He placed it gently on Cassie's head. "You can be the Dragon Princess on our float!"

The new Dragon Princess scooped up her little flower friend. "And I choose you, Cosmo, to be my flower," said Cassie.

"You mean I got picked?" asked Cosmo as his petals perked up.

"It just wouldn't be any fun without *you*," beamed Cassie.

When the float was finished, Cassie couldn't believe her eyes. "Wow!" she cried. "It looks just like a picture in my favorite storybook!"

As Ord pulled the float, Wheezie and Zak tapped out a terrific tune on their dragon scales.

"It's perfect!" cried Cassie. "Oh, I just love a parade!"

Ord pulled the float all the way back to the School in the Sky, where their wise teacher, Quetzal, was waiting.

"*Niños,* where have you been?" asked Quetzal. "I've been worried about you."

"We made our own parade!" said Cassie. "And this is our new friend, Cosmo."

"It is truly a beautiful float," said Quetzal as he shook Cosmo's little leaf of a hand. "If you hurry, you can find a place for it in the school parade."

Soon it was time for Max and Emmy to go back home. The children watched Cassie and Cosmo waving from their beautiful float as it slowly faded from sight.

Then, with a shower of sparkles, Max and Emmy began their magical journey out of Dragon Land and back to their own playroom...until next time.

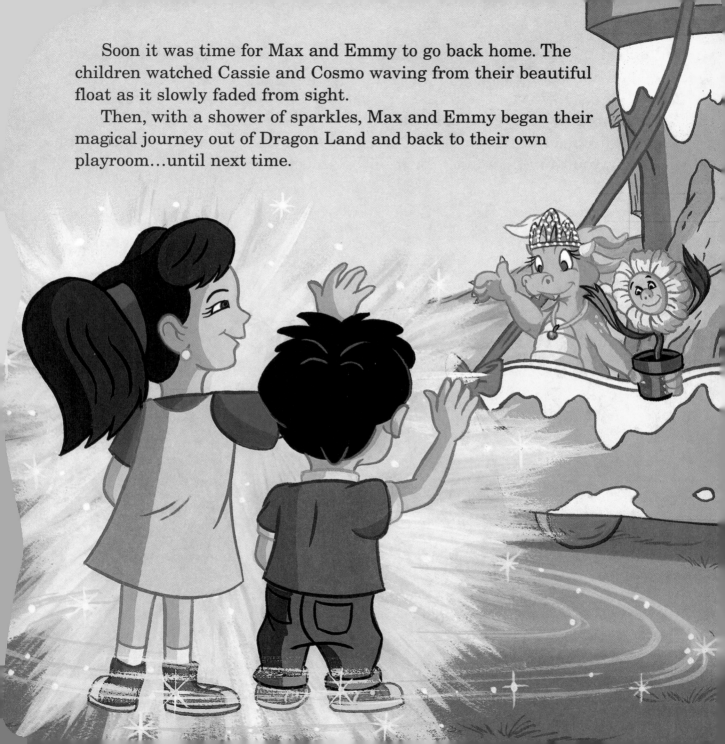